Sunny Acres was once the friendliest little farm in the co[u]... until the day that grumpy goat arrived.

GRUMPY

GOAT

by BRETT HELQUIST

HARPER

An Imprint of HarperCollinsPublishers

Goat had never had a single friend in his life.
He didn't want one now.
He was hungry. He was grumpy.
He didn't want to share.

When the pigs invited him to play, Goat chased them off.

Cow came to say hello. She left quickly.

The sheep just stayed away.

Goat never looked up at the blooming flowers or the green leaves or the bright sky. He never noticed the cool breeze or the warm sun. He just kept his head down, scowled, and ate.

He kicked down the garden fence and kept eating.

After finishing the cherries in the orchard,
Goat kept going. But at the top of Sunrise Hill . . .

Goat stopped.
What he saw reminded
him of something,

but he couldn't think what. He sat still and watched for a while.

Goat noticed that the ground was getting a little dry.
He got some water and then very carefully trimmed the grass.

Goat came back the next day, and the day after that.
He watered and trimmed. He sat and watched.

One curious sheep climbed halfway up the hill.
Goat eyed her suspiciously but didn't chase her away.

The next day, Cow wandered by. Goat let her help trim the grass.

The day after that,
the pigs dropped in for a game of tag.

Each evening Goat lay down to sleep on the top of the hill.
Each morning he woke up looking forward to seeing his friends again.

Until one day . . .

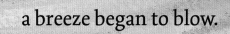a breeze began to blow.

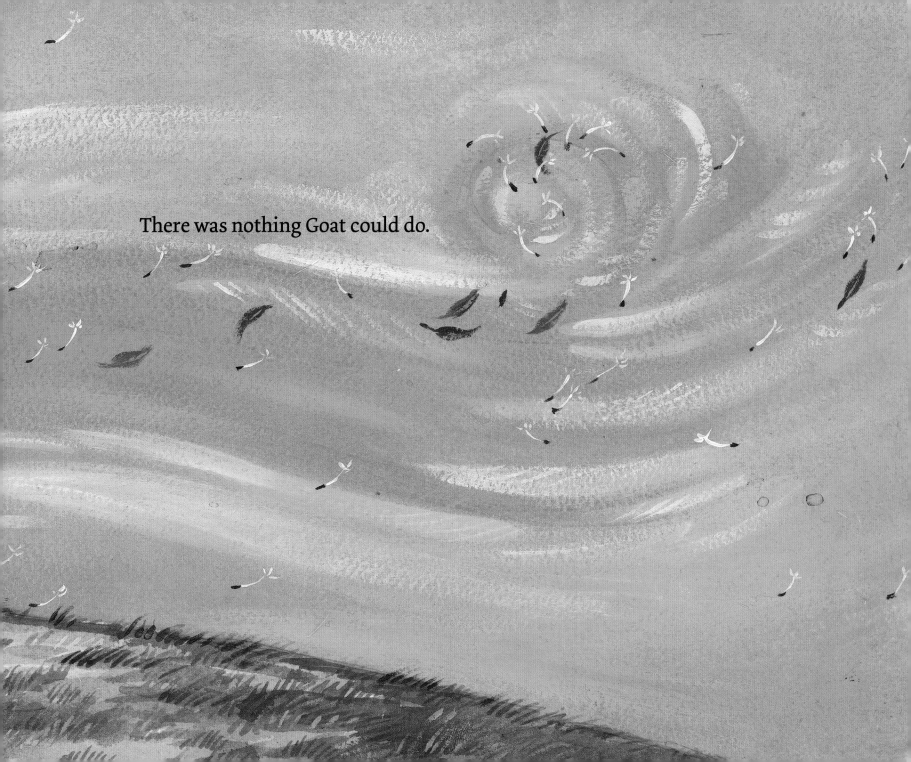

There was nothing Goat could do.

The pigs came by. Goat did not feel like playing, so they sat with him awhile.

Cow brought some nice hay. Goat wasn't hungry.

The sheep didn't know what to do, so they stayed nearby.

Goat spent long, lonely days and chilly nights on the top of the hill.
But his friends stayed close and visited often.

Until one day . . .

All summer long, Goat was happy to be at Sunny Acres . . .
once again the friendliest little farm in the county.

To my father, LaMar

Grumpy Goat
Copyright © 2013 by Brett Helquist

For information address HarperCollins Children's Books,
a division of HarperCollins Publishers,
10 East 53rd Street, New York, NY 10022.
www.harpercollinschildrens.com

Library of Congress Cataloging-in-Publication Data
Helquist, Brett.
Grumpy Goat / by Brett Helquist.—1st ed.
p. cm.
Summary: Goat is the grumpiest animal at Sunny Acres farm until
he remembers that there is more to life than eating and being alone.
ISBN 978-0-06-113953-6 (hardcover)
[1. Mood (Psychology)—Fiction. 2. Goats—Fiction.
3. Domestic animals—Fiction. 4. Farm life—Fiction.]
I. Title.
PZ7.H37598Gru 2013
[E]—dc23   2012011522

The artist used acrylic and oil on paper
to create the illustrations for this book.

Book design by Alison Donalty
12 13 14 15 16 SCP 10 9 8 7 6 5 4 3 2 1
❖ First Edition